Woodland Nutcracker

Avril Tyrrell

Illustrated by Frances Tyrrell

KPk
Key Porter Kids

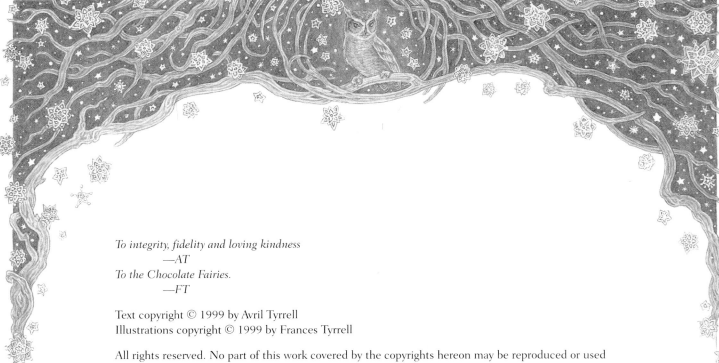

To integrity, fidelity and loving kindness
        —AT
To the Chocolate Fairies.
        —FT

Text copyright © 1999 by Avril Tyrrell
Illustrations copyright © 1999 by Frances Tyrrell

Canadian Cataloguing in Publication Data

Tyrrell, Avril, 1931–
        Woodland nutcracker

ISBN 1-55263-124-9

I. Tyrrell, Frances, 1959–   . II. Title.

PS8589.Y77W66 1999   jC813'.54   C99-931593-5
PZ7.T97Wo 1999

The publisher gratefully acknowledges the support of the
Canada Council for the Arts and the Ontario Arts Council for
its publishing program.

THE CANADA COUNCIL | LE CONSEIL DES ARTS
FOR THE ARTS | DU CANADA
SINCE 1957 | DEPUIS 1957

Canadä

We acknowledge the financial support of the Government of Canada through
the Book Publishing Industry Development Program (BPIDP) for our publishing
activities.

Key Porter kids
is an imprint of
Key Porter Books Limited
70 The Esplanade
Toronto, Ontario
Canada M5E 1R2

www.keyporter.com

Printed and bound in Italy
99 00 01 02 6 5 4 3 2 1

Long ago, far away from highways and city lights, where bright stars touched the tree tops and forest roots touched the edges of frozen lakes, a woodland family welcomed relatives and friends to a Christmas Eve party in their cosy island home.

Softly falling snowflakes drifted into the cottage as the guests arrived.

Clara and Peter had been busy all day, helping their parents. The table was laden with cookies, cakes, and candies. There were brightly wrapped parcels beneath a sparkling tree, and on the topmost branch was a shining star, made by Peter.

Grandpa arrived with hand-made gifts from his workshop: dancing puppets on strings, tin soldiers, and a handsome carved Nutcracker Bear.

Clara would always remember this happy evening: Grandpa's magic puppet show, Mother's paw-tapping fiddle music, the delicious supper, and, at last, the excitement of opening the parcels.

Peter and Cousin John decided to have a battle with the tin soldiers. "Nutcracker is my General," said Peter. "No, no, he is mine," cried both John and Clara. All three grabbed Nutcracker, and he fell to the floor with one leg in two pieces. The little bears cried. The party was spoiled.

"Now, now," growled Grandpa kindly, "wounded soldiers are always brave." The cubs stopped crying and watched as Grandpa took a little toolkit from his pocket, quickly and neatly mended Nutcracker's leg, and put him under the tree, "to rest."

"Time for little cubs to have a rest too," said the visiting parents, helping their tired cubs into warm boots and coats. "Thank you for a lovely party," they said and went home through the frosty night calling "Goodnight, goodnight, happy Christmas."

Late that night, everyone except Clara was asleep. "Perhaps Nutcracker can't sleep," she thought. "I'll bring him up here with me." She slipped out of bed, crept downstairs, and stopped in amazement at the living-room door.

The moonlit room was invaded by field mice. Some scampered across the supper table, filling little sacks with left-over party food. Others, armed with axes and bows and arrows, stood guard upon the floor. The tin soldiers, led by Nutcracker, marched towards them. This would be a fierce battle. The tiny weapons were needle sharp.

In her little bare paws, Clara stepped bravely between the two armies. "Truce," she cried, waving a white table napkin, "no one fights on Christmas Eve. The mice are hungry, the food is for their children."

Nutcracker, the soldiers, and the brave but frightened mice put down their weapons.

"We have plenty of food. Help me fill their sacks," said Clara. The mice soon left, happily laden, into the icy night. "Thank you. You are so kind! Happy Christmas," they squeaked.

Clara felt sleepy and decided to go back to bed. But the moonlight was much brighter now. The Christmas tree was growing larger and real snowflakes drifted through its branches. Where was Nutcracker? What was happening?

"Brave, kind Clara," growled a deep voice. She turned and Nutcracker stood before her, no longer made of wood, but a live fur-and-claws bear. He was tall, and so handsome.

"You knew the power of the Christmas Truce, Clara," said Nutcracker, "so this night you are to be the guest of honour at the palace of the great bear, Ursa Major. Come, I am your escort."

He took her paw in his and led her to the tree. The branches parted; they walked through and were out on the shore of the frozen lake.

Snowflakes danced around them as they stepped onto the ice, where a fantastic air balloon was moored. Smartly dressed attendants helped them on board and cast off the ropes. Up and away they floated, and Clara looked down at her island home growing smaller and farther away. Where were they going? "Look up," said Nutcracker.

Clara looked in wonder as they sailed through the dancing Northern Lights and into the Milky Way. At last the balloon began to descend. It bounced gently and came to rest near a palace of ice in a great circle of light, directly under the path of the Pole Star.

Moonbeams shone around the majestic great bear, Ursa Major, who was waiting to greet them. "We are honoured to have you with us, dear Clara," she said graciously, "and so pleased to see you again, Prince Nutcracker."

Clara was nearly overcome with shyness, but managed to be polite and shake the queen's great paw. They were led into the glittering palace and they sat beside Ursa Major on crystal thrones.

Ursa Major raised her paw, and all was silent as her little page, Ursa Minor, read a Proclamation.

"This night we honour Clara, the Peacemaker, for her great courage and kindness in bringing about a Christmas Truce. At the request of our great queen, Ursa Major, we present Le Cirque des Étoiles! We begin with a dramatic flamenco presentation by the renowned young spectacled bears, Rosa and Paco from Mexico."

The paw-stamping, castanet-clicking, swirling dance ended all too soon, but then, to Clara's delight, Rosa and Paco came and sat at her feet on the steps to the thrones.

Clara was too shy to say a word, but she nodded politely and listened as Rosa and Paco told her about the next dancer, Sarita Thapa, a lesser panda from Nepal.

To a chinkle of little bells, Sarita danced before the thrones. She was more beautiful and graceful than Clara had imagined possible.

When her dance was over, Sarita too came and sat at Clara's feet. She spoke in such a friendly way that Clara was reminded of a line from her mother's favourite song: "*for beauty lives with kindness.*"

"Now Clara," laughed Sarita, "this next performance is by the famous jugglers, Tung Tung and Chi Chi from China. Don't try it at home with your mother's teacups!"

Two giant pandas trotted into the pavilion. There on the ice they placed a little table set with fine china. Clara watched in amazement as they began to toss the cups and saucers into the air. What would her mother say? The cups, saucers, teapot, and lid flew between the huge paws of the magnificent bears, but not one piece was broken.

Clara's paws grew tired from clapping. She wanted to remember everything to tell Peter, but would he believe her?

No time to worry now: Ursa Minor was announcing the next act. "From the Arctic Circle, Yuk Tuk, Olympian Gymnast, presents her prize-winning ribbon routine."

A young polar bear entered, swirling a starry ribbon. Moving nimbly on her great paws, she never once let the ribbon droop, but swung it smoothly into dancing patterns of loops, spirals, and figures of eight. Clara wondered, "Could I try this at home?"

"Now, a tribute from your woodland friends," announced Ursa Major. "They really wanted to be here tonight."

Clara heard the music of her father's favourite tune, "The Black Bear." Into the palace, playing the pipes and drums she knew so well, marched the mice and squirrels from her island home.

All the bears stood up to applaud at the end of the performance. "A standing ovation," cried Nutcracker. Clara felt proud, and just a bit homesick.

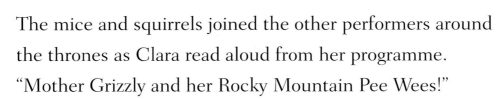

The mice and squirrels joined the other performers around the thrones as Clara read aloud from her programme. "Mother Grizzly and her Rocky Mountain Pee Wees!"

A huge grizzly bear skated to the foot of the thrones and curtsied. She blew six times upon a whistle and from beneath her great red and white skirt emerged six cubs with hockey sticks. With Mother Grizzly as referee, the cubs skated a mock practice session. They chased one another, misbehaved, and two were even sent to the penalty box.

Clara joined in the laughter and applause, but suddenly felt homesick once again. This place was exciting and wonderful, but home was for always.

"The last act, Clara," said Ursa Major kindly. "Look up."

Clara looked up and saw two swings hanging from the
icy dome. On each swing were two little koala bears. "From
Australia, Bottlebrush and Orchid, Billy Buttons and
Bluebell, Stellar Trapeze Artistes," announced Ursa Minor.

Fearlessly the koalas swung and somersaulted high above
the thrones. There was great applause as they slid down ropes
of flowers to take a final bow with the other performers.

"Time to go home now, Clara," said Nutcracker. "It is
nearly Christmas morning."

"Yes, I must go now," agreed Clara. She was so sleepy she could hardly say, "Good-bye, and thank you so much!"

Ursa Major, Ursa Minor, and all the performers escorted Clara and Nutcracker back to the magical balloon. "Will Peter believe me when I tell him about this?" she cried.

"There is a special present under the tree for Peter," said Ursa Major. "I have marked it with a star. You will remember. You will tell him, and he will believe you."

Long ago, far away from highways and city lights, where bright stars touched the tree tops and forest roots touched the edges of frozen lakes, two little bears sat on the steps of their woodland home. They were looking at the sky through a beautiful telescope, marked with a shining star.